Bo and the Dragon-Pup

Read more
UNICORN DIARIES
books!

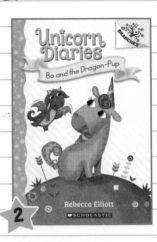

Unicorn Diaries

Bo and the Dragon-Pup

Rebecca Elliott

~BRANCHES~
SCHOLASTIC INC.

For Kirsty.
May you always believe unicorns are real. X – R.E.

Special thanks to Kyle Reed
for his contributions to this book.

Library of Congress Cataloging-in-Publication Data Names: Elliott, Rebecca, author.
Title: Bo and the dragon-pup / Rebecca Elliott.
Description: First edition. | New York, NY : Branches/Scholastic Inc., 2020.
| Series: Unicorn diaries ; 2 | Summary: Rainbow Tinseltail (called Bo)
has never actually seen a dragon, but when things start going missing from
Sparklegrove School for Unicorns all clues seem to point to a dragon-pup
called Scorch—but when Scorch does not return to the dragon caves, Bo and the other
unicorns become worried that he has gotten lost in the forest and they
set out to find their new friend.
Identifiers: LCCN 2019007658| ISBN 9781338323382 (pbk. : alk. paper) |
ISBN 9781338323405 (hardcover : alk. paper)
Subjects: LCSH: Unicorns—Juvenile fiction. | Dragons—Juvenile fiction. |
Magic—Juvenile fiction. | Friendship–Juvenile fiction. |
Diaries—Juvenile fiction. | CYAC: Unicorns—Fiction. | Dragons—Fiction.
| Magic—Fiction. | Friendship—Fiction. | Diaries—Fiction. | LCGFT: Diary fiction.
Classification: LCC PZ7.E45812 Bk 2020 | DDC [Fic]—dc23
LC record available at https://lccn.loc.gov/2019007658)

10 9 8 7 6 5 4 3 2 1   20 21 22 23 24

Printed in China 62
First edition, March 2020

Edited by Katie Carella
Book design by Maria Mercado

Table of Contents

Hello!

Sunday

Hello, Diary!

It's me again! Rainbow Tinseltail! But you can call me Bo.

I wonder what adventures we'll have in Sparklegrove Forest this week!

By the way, Sparklegrove Forest is where I live. Here it is:

Rainbow Falls

Troll Caves

Glimmer Glade

Sparklegrove School for Unicorns

Dragon Nests

Budbloom Meadow

Snowbelle Mountain

Unipods

Fairy Village

Twinkleplop
Lagoon

Goblin
Castle

Lots of magical creatures live here . . .

Like dragons! Truth is, I've never actually seen a dragon. But here are four things I know:

Dragons live in nests.

They love throwing rocks.

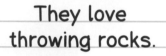

They breathe fire.

They only eat food the color of fire (like red tomatoes, sunny oranges, and yellow custard).

But enough about dragons.

As you can see, I am a unicorn.

Horn
Good for reading in the dark!

Rainbow Mane
Can store lots of stuff!

Tummy
Filled with brightly
colored food!

Hooves
Rainbows shoot out of them
when we dance!

Unicorns are much more than a glowing horn. Here are some fun **UNI-FACTS**:

We each have a different Unicorn Power. I'm a Wish Unicorn.

I can grant one wish every week!

We sneeze glitter.

ACHOO!

We live together in **UNIPODS**.

We're not good at doing cartwheels.

OOF!

I love Sparklegrove School for Unicorns! S.S.U. is my school and my home.

This is my BEST friend Sunny Huckleberry. He is a Crystal Clear Unicorn. He can turn invisible!

Here are all my friends and our teacher.

Jed   Nutmeg   Piper   Mr. Rumptwinkle

Scarlett   Sunny   Me   Monty

Check out their **TWINKLE-TASTIC** powers!

Healer
Unicorn

Thingamabob
Unicorn

Flying
Unicorn

Weather
Unicorn

Size-Changer
Unicorn

Shape-Shifter
Unicorn

We study **GLITTERRIFIC** subjects, like:

MAGICAL CREATURES

COLORFUL COOKERY

HORN CARE

$$1+1+1+1+1=$$

MATH

My friends and I each have a special unicorn patch blanket. The patches show everything we've learned so far. Every week, Mr. Rumptwinkle tells us what new patch we're going to try to earn. Then we work hard all week for it!

I can't wait to find out what this week's patch will be!

2

Unicorn Detectives

Diary, my friends and I made a SHOCKING discovery this morning! When we woke up, Monty's patch blanket was MISSING!

Don't worry Monty, we'll help you find it.

I definitely had it with me when I went to sleep.

We searched our unipod.

Then we all searched the forest near our school.

But we couldn't find it anywhere!

We trotted over to Mr. Rumptwinkle to tell him the bad news. And we saw something else super shocking!

Mr. Rumptwinkle! Your glasses look, um, different. Where are your normal ones?

Good question! My glasses were on my nightstand when I went to bed. But when I woke up, they were gone! So I'm wearing an old pair.

Your glasses are missing, too?

We told Mr. Rumptwinkle about Monty's blanket. Then we checked to see if anything else was missing.

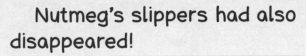

Nutmeg's slippers had also disappeared!

A missing patch blanket! Missing glasses! AND missing slippers! A thief must have snuck in while we were asleep!

But who would steal that kind of stuff?

That is the perfect question to start off our week, Scarlett! You see, this week will be the DETECTIVE patch week! Work together to solve this mystery, and you will all get a new patch at the Patch Parade on Friday.

Scarlett used her thingamabob power to magic up detective hats and magnifying glasses for all of us.

Then we looked for clues. I found the first one!

The small window at the top of our unipod was open.

The thief must be someone who can jump up high!

Or someone really tall.

Or someone who can fly.

Later, Monty found another clue.

We studied the crumbs.

We studied our MAGICAL CREATURES books while we ate lunch.

Carrots are orange . . .

Orange is the color of fire!

And who eats fiery-colored foods?!

GASP!

DRAGONS!

We quickly came up with a plan.

Let's go on a dragon hunt tomorrow!

That sounds dangerous. Maybe we should ask Mr. Rumptwinkle?

No. If we want our new patch, we're going to have to solve this mystery on our own.

Jed is right. Besides, we won't get close to the dragons.

We'll just spy on them to see if they have our stuff. Then we'll tell Mr. Rumptwinkle!

Sunny and I were too excited to sleep. We've never even gone <u>near</u> a dragon nest before!

I wonder what the dragons will look like.

I bet they're HUGE and MEAN!

Oh, don't say that. I don't want to go if it's too scary.

Don't worry, Bo. We'll be together.

Diary, I can't wait for the dragon hunt!

3

The Dragon Hunt

Tuesday

We woke up early to search for dragons.

We followed the footprints until they stopped.

Great. What do we do now?

Suddenly, Nutmeg called down to us.

The leaves on these treetops are burned!

We stared up at the trees above.

I bet a FIRE-BREATHING dragon did that!

There are <u>lots</u> of burned leaves!

Lead the way, Nutmeg!

We trotted deep into the forest until
we heard a big **ROAR**! Orange flames
shot up into the sky!

We ducked behind some rocks and
peeked over to see –

Three HUGE dragons! They were
breathing fire and throwing rocks. We'd
found the dragon nests!

We were all a bit scared. My hooves
were shaking!

We whispered to one another.

Wow. Dragons are much bigger than I thought they would be.

There's no way those dragons could fit through our unipod window.

You're right. It was silly to think a dragon was the thief.

Great! Can we go home now?

Okay. Let's go home.

As Jed was leading the way home,
Piper yelped and leaped into the air.

We looked around.

There's no one else here.

Maybe you're just feeling jumpy after seeing those scary dragons?

I KNOW somebody pulled my tail!

We kept trotting through the forest. But soon, more strange things happened.

A big bunch of leaves flew into Monty's face.

We heard giggling in the trees above.

Suddenly, a DRAGON leaped out in front of us!

ROAR!!!

Then we saw it was only a little dragon-pup! He rolled around on the ground, laughing!

I looked at the dragon-pup and realized three things:

1. This little dragon could fly.

2. He was small enough to fit through our **UNIPOD** window.

3. He was chewing on a carrot!

YOU'RE who we've been looking for!

The dragon-pup smiled and flapped his wings. It seemed like he wanted us to play with him.

I bet you can't catch me!

Come back here!

We spent the rest of the day chasing the little dragon through the forest. He was fast and very good at hiding!

Sometimes he'd sneak up on us, then fly off again.

Ugh! Quit pulling my tail!

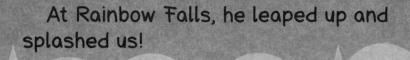

At Rainbow Falls, he leaped up and splashed us!

This is silly.

SPLASH!

We're too tired to catch him now.

And it's getting late.

We decided to go home and try again tomorrow.

That dragon-pup is so naughty!

He is. But what if he's not the thief?

Huh?

Well, why would a dragon-pup want <u>our</u> stuff?

Hmmm. I'm not sure. Let's rethink all of our clues.

We kept thinking about the clues. And at **CLOUDTIME**, Sunny shared a new idea about the thief.

Now I'm worried we might not solve the mystery and earn our DETECTIVE patches. Oh Diary, I don't know what to think! We all went to sleep feeling very confused.

The Trap

This morning, we trotted back to the dragon nests.

> Keep your eyes open for Monty's blanket, Mr. Rumptwinkle's eyeglasses, and Nutmeg's slippers! If we see the dragon-pup with any of our stuff, we'll <u>know</u> he is the thief.

> Be on the lookout for rabbits, too!

Sunny and Monty used their powers so they could creep close enough to hear the dragons.

Then they galloped back to us.

We ate lunch at Glimmer Glade. We were all worried about the little dragon, even if it did turn out that he had taken our things.

This is all our fault.

We need to bring Scorch home to his family.

But how will we find him?

If Scorch **is** the thief, then I think I know how to bring him out of hiding. We will make **him** find **us**!

We trotted to Rainbow Falls, where we last saw Scorch. Then we made a big pile of our detective hats and magnifying glasses.

I hope our things will attract the thief!

Sunny and Monty used their powers again, so they could hide close to the pile. They were ready to catch the thief!

It was a **SPARKLE-TASTIC** plan. Right, Diary? And it worked! Just not quite how I'd expected . . .

But as Sunny and Monty stepped back, we saw who they had caught. And it wasn't Scorch.

So the thief WAS a rabbit!

But Piper wasn't quite right either, because this rabbit was not <u>really</u> a rabbit. It was actually Mr. Rumptwinkle!

Right away, we earned our DETECTIVE patches!

It usually feels great when we earn a new patch. But this time it didn't feel so good. We all felt bad about chasing Scorch when he wasn't really the thief.

Mr. Rumptwinkle asked what was wrong. So we told him about the carrot clue we got wrong, about our dragon hunt, and about Scorch going missing.

Scorch's family is really worried about him.

Oh dear. I didn't realize you were all out chasing dragons! You were very brave. It looks like your next job as detectives is to figure out how to make things right.

We put our hats back on and talked on the way back to our unipod.

We need to find Scorch!

We need to bring that dragon-pup home!

I hope Scorch is all right, Diary. Yes he's a bit naughty, but he's only a little dragon. We MUST find him tomorrow!

The Missing Dragon-Pup

Thursday

This morning, we searched the forest for hours. Finally, we spotted small dragon footprints and followed them to Fairy Village.

Hello, fairies! Have you seen a dragon-pup?

As we trotted along, we met other creatures who had seen Scorch.

A pesky little dragon threw me up in the air like I was a beach ball! Then he giggled and flew that way.

A sneaky dragon-pup tagged my belly and said, "You can't catch me!" Then he giggled and flew that way.

At last, we found Scorch!

I went and sat with him.

Hi, Scorch! I'm Bo!

We all told him our names.

Did you get lost because we chased you?

What? No.

Then why haven't you gone home?

And why have you been causing trouble all over the forest?

Scorch told us that he wasn't trying to run away or be naughty . . .

He just wanted someone to play with!

Don't your big brothers and sister play with you?

No. They're too busy being grown-up dragons. All they do now is throw rocks and breathe fire.

Why don't you join in?

I'm too small to throw rocks. All I can throw are tiny pebbles. And I can't even breathe fire yet.

We told Scorch his family missed him and was worried about him.

I'd like to go home. But now I'm not sure which way it is.

We'll take you.

Come on! Catch us if you can!

Sunny whispered to me as we raced Scorch to the dragon nests.

Are you scared about meeting the big dragons?

A bit. I hope they won't blame us for Scorch running off.

The dragons weren't scary at all!
They were just <u>so</u> happy to see Scorch!

They gave us big dragon hugs, too.

Thank you so much for bringing Scorch home!

You're welcome.

The dragons uncovered something **TWINKLE-TASTIC**!

Scorch asked us to play with him.
So we played together until sunset.
And we invited him to our Patch Parade
tomorrow. He said yes — YAY!

6

Rainbow Rain

Friday

Everyone was super excited for the Patch Parade. When Scorch arrived, we trotted right over to him.

Did your brothers and sister play with you today, Scorch?

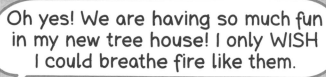

Oh yes! We are having so much fun in my new tree house! I only WISH I could breathe fire like them.

Sunny gave me a wink. Then I knew just what to do! I swished my tail . . .

Suddenly, Scorch breathed huge rainbow-colored flames!

We paraded past Mr. Rumptwinkle
and collected our DETECTIVE patches.

I'm very proud of you. You were all great
detectives this week. And you were
great friends to a dragon-pup.

Mr. Rumptwinkle gave a special patch to Scorch!

This is a PLAY patch. It means you can play with the unicorns any time — so long as you behave yourself!

Thank you! And don't worry, I am never naughty!

But then Scorch got SO excited that he accidentally breathed flames that set fire to the parade decorations!

Jed used his Unicorn Power to make it rain. He put out the fire in no time. But Scorch's magic flames made the rain turn rainbow-colored! So we all danced in the rain!

Phew! This has been a **GLITTERRIFIC** week! We all have a new patch AND a fiery new friend!

See you next time, Diary!

Rebecca Elliott may not have a magical horn or sneeze glitter, but she's still a lot like a unicorn. Rebecca always tries to have a positive attitude, she likes to laugh a lot, and she lives with some great creatures — her guitar-playing husband, noisy-yet-charming children, crazy chickens, and a big, lazy cat called Bernard. She gets to hang out with these fun characters and write stories for a living, so she thinks her life is pretty magical!

Rebecca is the author of JUST BECAUSE, MR. SUPER POOPY PANTS, and the *USA Today* bestselling early chapter book series OWL DIARIES.

Unicorn Diaries

How much do you know about Bo and the Dragon-Pup?

Sunny and Monty sneak up to the big dragons to hear what they are saying. How do their special Unicorn Powers help them stay hidden?

The unicorns talk to lots of different creatures when they're looking for Scorch (turn to pages 55–57). Make a list of all the creatures they meet.

Think about a time when someone was too busy to play with you. How did it make you feel? What did you do next?

The unicorns are scared to meet the dragons. Should they be worried? What are the dragons really like?

Scorch's family built him a tree house! Draw and label a tree house you would like to play in. Would it have a swing, like Scorch's?